The Other Ducks

Ellen Yeomans   Pictures by Chris Sheban

A NEAL PORTER BOOK
ROARING BROOK PRESS
NEW YORK

This one is for Mom and Dad who mostly managed to keep their ducks in a row. —E.Y.

To the duck I ate that one time. I'm sorry. —C.S.

Text copyright © 2018 by Ellen Yeomans
Illustrations copyright © 2018 by Chris Sheban
A Neal Porter Book
Published by Roaring Brook Press
Roaring Brook Press is a division of Holtzbrinck Publishing Holdings Limited Partnership
175 Fifth Avenue, New York, NY 10010
The art for this book was created using watercolor, colored pencil, and graphite.
mackids.com

Library of Congress Control Number: 2017957295
ISBN: 978-1-62672-502-7

Our books may be purchased in bulk for promotional, educational, or business use. Please
contact your local bookseller or the Macmillan Corporate and Premium Sales Department
at (800) 221-7945 ext. 5442 or by e-mail at MacmillanSpecialMarkets@macmillan.com.

First edition 2018
Printed in China by RR Donnelley Asia Printing Solutions Ltd., Dongguan City, Guangdong Province
1 3 5 7 9 10 8 6 4 2

This Duck and That Duck were the best of friends.

They played all spring as
the rushes grew high and lush
beside the wadey-water of
the Little Puddle.

One day,
This Duck
and That
Duck went
waddling
through the
rushes.

"At a time like this there should be Other Ducks," This Duck said.

"What's Other Ducks?" That Duck asked.

"Like us, only not us," This Duck answered. "If there were Other Ducks, we would waddle in a line."

"Aren't we in a line? After all, I go where you go," That Duck said.

This Duck stopped. "Two is not a line. Two is a *follow*. A line is better. A line is more ducky. We need Other Ducks for that. Right now, we're just a couple of ducks out for a waddle."

They continued waddling in a not-quite-line until they came to a Big Puddle full of cool, clear, wallow-water.

This Duck splashed and splished,
she dipped and dunked.
"I'm swimming!" she called.
"How do you know?" That
Duck asked.

"It just feels like swimming,"
This Duck answered.

That Duck dipped his webbed foot into the Big Puddle and pulled it right back out.

"And what exactly is swimming?" That Duck asked.

"This," said This Duck. "It's like waddling but in the water. I don't think my feet are touching bottom."

"Not touching? Oh dear!" That Duck fretted.

This Duck looked down to check and saw . . .
another duck looking up at her.

"Come on in!" This Duck called to That
Duck. "There's a wonderful surprise in here!"

"Is it safe? That's an awfully big puddle."

That Duck was worried but finally flip-flap
followed. He paddled and paddled, and then looked
down to see if his feet were touching the bottom
and saw . . . another duck looking up at him.

"Are these—?" That Duck began.
"The Other Ducks," This Duck finished.

As summer warmed the world around them, The Other Ducks swam whenever and wherever This Duck and That Duck swam. They dipped and dunked at the same time, too.

If only The Other Ducks weren't always upside down. And though This Duck and That Duck tried, they could never get The Other Ducks behind them so they could all swim in a line.

They never waddled in a line, either, because
The Other Ducks never got out of the Big Puddle.
It was nice to have them around, but it was not
as ducky as it might have been.

And then one windy, rainy day The Other Ducks disappeared.
This Duck and That Duck called and called for them.
They swam through the choppy water
to the far side of the
Big Puddle. But
they didn't
find them.

The next day was sunny and bright and The Other Ducks
were back. Soon, autumn claimed the world all
around them. More and more days were
windy, rainy, and cold. The
Other Ducks were
not there as often.

One day, This Duck said, "I think they've left us."

"Is that them?" That Duck asked.

"Bug," said
This Duck.

"Is that them?" That Duck asked.
"Falling leaves," This Duck said. She
was beginning to wonder if That Duck
had learned anything all summer.

"How about that?" That Duck asked.

"Birdy-bird," This Duck answered.

"How do you know?" That Duck asked.

"It just looks like a birdy-bird." This Duck stretched her wings and pretended to be a birdy-bird.

"What do they do?" asked That Duck, pretending the same thing.

"They fly high and they fly far," This Duck said.

And then, This Duck ran . . .

and . . . flew.

and hopped . . .

"Look! My feet aren't touching. Be a birdy-bird, too,"
This Duck called down.

And though That Duck wasn't at all sure
he wanted to be one, he ran and hopped
and flew. This Duck and That Duck flew
around their Big Puddle. They searched
for The Other Ducks but they did not
see them. Still, the flying was fun.

One day, This Duck did not want to play with That Duck. She was restless. "My feathers itch," she said.

The next day That Duck felt the very same way.

"We need to go," This Duck said.

"Where to?" That Duck asked.

"To South."

"Where is that?"

"We'll figure it out."

That Duck looked into the Big Puddle. "I wish The Other Ducks could go with us."

"Maybe The Other Ducks are already there," This Duck said. "Let's fly instead of waddle."

"Because we don't quite make a line?" That Duck asked.

"Yes, and because I think we need to get to South faster," This Duck said. "Look, so many birdy-birds. Let's follow them to South."

This Duck and That Duck took to
the air right behind the birdy-birds.
When they caught up, they found
that the birdy-birds were . . .
Other Ducks!

This Duck and That Duck
joined a line. A line!
"Like us, only not us," This Duck
called to That Duck. And all
together they flew to South.

Winter settled itself over the
Big Puddle and the Little Puddle,
but there weren't any ducks to see
it, or feel it, or hear how very
quiet it was.

When spring arrived, This Duck and
That Duck flew home.
   This time, as the rushes grew tall
and lush beside the Little Puddle, a
lively line formed behind them.

This Duck led the way to the Big Puddle.
"Keep the line, everyone," she called.
"Why are they so small?" That Duck asked.

"It's the way everything starts," This Duck answered.
"How do you know?" That Duck asked.
"I just pay attention," This Duck said.

This Duck and That Duck and The Little Other Ducks
waddled in a line to the cool, clear, wallow-water. And
every single one of them felt downright ducky.